A PET FOR BABAR

Adapted by
Lesley Young

One morning Flora was very sad. One of her pet goldfish had died.

"Did you ever have a goldfish that died?" she asked, looking sadly at her remaining pet.

"No," said Babar, "but once I had to give up a pet I really loved. It all started when Rataxes, the Rhino King, tried to stir up trouble in Celesteville…"

In the palace, Cornelius was crossly pacing up and down. "This is dreadful," said Pompadour, "it's very disturbing."

"Disturbing?" roared Cornelius. "Why, it's diabolical, it's…" He spluttered down his trunk looking for the word.

"It's a blockade," said Pompadour.

"What's a blockade?" asked Babar.

"A blockade is the blocking of certain goods to prevent them getting to those who need them," said Pompadour.

"In this case, us," added Cornelius.

"But what is Rataxes keeping from us?" asked Babar. "Fuel? Medical supplies?"

"Much worse," said Cornelius. "Pomegranates!"

"Pomegranates?" said Babar in disbelief.

Cornelius picked one up from a bowl on Babar's desk. "This is the last pomegranate in the kingdom!"

"But why are pomegranates so important?" asked Babar at last.

Pompadour strutted over, took the pomegranate from Cornelius and dropped it in disgust. "Although I detest the fruit it plays a vital part in the livelihood of your subjects. No pomegranates means no pomegranate juice makers, and that means a loss of vitamin C and Riboflavin."

"My tusks!" cried Babar. "I can't let Rataxes get away with this!"

In the Rhino Palace, Rataxes was at his desk surrounded by piles of pomegranates.

"But what's so important about pomegranates?" Basil was asking.

"Nothing, Basil," said Rataxes. "It's the blockade that matters. Pomegranates are just the start of my plan to control Celesteville!"

Just then the door burst open and Muffy, the pet warthog, bounded in, followed by Lady Rataxes. Rataxes took a flying leap out of the way.

"You're getting him all excited," said Lady Rataxes. "He wants his walkies."

Muffy snapped and growled below Rataxes. "Why can't Basil take him?" he asked, then **"OUCH!"** as Muffy's teeth took a chunk out of the seat of his trousers.

"That was my last uniform!" he cried, falling into the pomegranates. Muffy dashed out of the way.

"You nearly squashed my baby!" said Lady Rataxes, angrily.

"Here," she commanded, "take Muffy for his walk. She gave his lead to Rataxes. The warthog ran outside, dragging a desperate Rataxes along behind him.

"He wants to be friends with you," called Lady Rataxes, as the warthog snarled and bared his teeth.

"Basil, don't leave me..." shouted Rataxes as he was pulled through the pomegranates.

In Babar's office, Cornelius was pacing up and down. "Please think again, Your Majesty. I'm sure we could bargain with Rataxes. We could exchange something."

"But Cornelius," said Babar, "they're *our* pomegranates. Why should we reward someone for stealing them from us?"

"We'll have to," said Cornelius.

Elephants could be heard outside. "Give us back our pomegranates!" "We want action!"

"I can't think here," said Babar. "I must find some peace and quiet."

Meanwhile, in the jungle, Rataxes was complaining. Behind him came Basil and Muffy. The warthog was trying to reach Rataxes.

"I've got a blockade to run," muttered Rataxes, and stopped in his tracks. **"OUCH!"** Muffy sank his teeth firmly into the seat of Rataxes' trousers.

"You didn't say you were going to stop!" said Basil.

Rataxes lifted Basil by the lapels. "That's the last bite of me he's going to get. Take Muffy for a walk, Basil. A long walk on a short path!"

Basil looked at him in horror. "You don't mean leave the poor little thing in the jungle, do you?" One look at Rataxes' face was enough.

Basil padded through the jungle with Muffy. He found a strong tree and tied the lead to it. "Sorry," he said, "but you heard him."

Then he heard someone coming. With a last wave, Basil dashed into the bushes.

In the jungle, Babar tripped over Muffy's lead and landed on the ground. Muffy leapt on top of him and began to lick him all over.

"Where did you come from?" asked Babar. "Oh - your lead has got tied to this tree." He untied Muffy. "You can go home now."

Muffy didn't budge. "You're lost!" said Babar. "I'll take you home and find you something to eat."

Basil watched them. "Wait till I tell Rataxes," he chuckled.

In Celesteville, the pomegranate panic was reaching new heights.

"We *must* make a deal with Rataxes," said Cornelius. "I've done the paperwork."

Just then Muffy dashed in, scattering the papers. "Perhaps you are too busy to have a new pet," suggested Cornelius.

Babar was patting Muffy. "We'll think of something, won't we boy?"

"He's taken the warthog as an adviser!" groaned Pompadour.

Back at the Rhino Palace, Lady Rataxes was *not* happy. "I'm sorry, my sweet," said Rataxes. "He broke his lead and ran off. I charged after him, risking life and limb, but there was no sign…"

Then he added, "You can have another pet. Something without teeth - I mean, teething troubles."

Lady Rataxes dropped limply on to a chair. She sobbed, "I want my Muffy. There is nothing I love so much, except you, and if you are still the man I married you'll bring him back to me!"

Rataxes backed out of the room, saying, "Of course, dear, of course!" He backed straight into Basil who had been listening.

"Muffy is in Celesteville," said Basil. "We shall have to steal him back."

"Let's go," growled Rataxes.

Babar and Muffy were playing in the palace gardens. They didn't notice that two bushes seemed to be following them.

"Fetch!" cried Babar, throwing a stick. Muffy followed it into the larger bush. **"OUCH!"**

Muffy reappeared with a patch of ripped cloth in his teeth, then licked Babar's face. "Are you hungry again?" said Babar. "Stay here - I'll fetch you some scraps."

Rataxes called, "I've come to take you home to mummy." Muffy snarled and leapt into the bush.

Babar was returning with the food when he saw Muffy chasing two bushes out of the garden. As he watched, the bushes jumped over the fence. There was a giant splash.

"Oh how I hate that hog!" cried Rataxes from the palace fountain.

"Rataxes!" called Babar. "What are you doing here?"

Babar held Muffy who growled and tried to reach Rataxes.

"I thought you'd be too busy with your blockade to pay a social call," said Babar to Rataxes, taking the two rhinos up to his office.

"What blockade?" asked Rataxes, innocently. Babar pointed at a solitary pomegranate.

"Oh - heh, heh - that blockade..."

"That blockade," said Babar. "And now I'm calling the guards."

"Wait!" said Basil. "The reason Lord Rataxes has come here is to talk about ending the blockade." Basil was playing for time. "We will lift the blockade in exchange for... for...well..."

"WHAT, Basil?" snapped Rataxes.

"Feathers!" cried Basil. "One thousand pounds of feathers!"

"No gold?" asked Rataxes. "And no land, or anything?"

"No - you're happy with feathers."

"Feathers..." repeated Rataxes in amazement.

Later, in the guest chamber, Rataxes asked Basil, "Why do I want all those feathers?"

"You don't want them, Your Righness," Basil replied.

Rataxes grabbed Basil by the lapels and pinned him on his horn. "Then tell me what I *do* want, Basil," he said coldly.

"You want to get Muffy back," said Basil, "and this is a trick."

Rataxes beamed and let Basil go. "I thought that's what I wanted!"

Meanwhile, Babar was looking for Muffy. "Time for your bath," he said. At the word 'bath', Muffy ran off. Babar went in search of him.

"Oh Muffy!" came a voice. Muffy turned to see a figure that looked like Lady Rataxes. As he watched, it walked towards him, tripped over the long dress and fell. "I've got you some beastie bites."

Muffy trotted up to the figure. To his horror, Rataxes' arm appeared and snapped on a lead. "Got you!"

"Miserable little hairball!" muttered Rataxes. "You won't get away again." For a moment Muffy was stunned, then he jumped out of Rataxes' arms and bolted, with Rataxes still holding on to the lead.

"BAAS-ILLL!!!" yelled Rataxes. "WHOAH BOY! WHOAH MUFFY!"

Basil chased after them. "Reel him in, Your Righness!"

In a nearby courtyard, Pompadour and Cornelius were gathering the feathers. A long line of naked jungle birds watched as Pompadour checked off his list. "Well, that's it - one thousand pounds exactly."

Cornelius stepped forward and spoke. "On behalf of His Majesty, I would like to thank you all for your help, your patriotism, and your..."

"Feathers?" suggested Pompadour.

The birds didn't get a chance to reply. There was a yelp and Muffy appeared. They watched in horror as he dragged Rataxes through the mound of feathers.

Muffy dragged Rataxes on to the courtyard and into the fountain with a giant splash. Cornelius, Pompadour and Babar arrived on the scene. "We do have an indoor bath," said Pompadour, smoothly.

Muffy leapt back into Babar's arms and licked his face. "We're so sorry about this," said Cornelius to Rataxes, "but I hope you noticed we *had* your feathers ready."

"Not so fast!" said Rataxes.

"If it's your dress that worries you," said Pompadour, "we'll have it cleaned..."

Basil was thinking fast. "Actually, I distinctly remember Lord Rataxes asked for *fuschia* feathers."

The elephants gazed at him in amazement. "Of course," agreed Rataxes. "Ordinary feathers are two a penny. What do you take me for - a fool?"

"That wasn't part of the deal and you know it," said Babar.

"Well, you can take it or leave it," said Rataxes, and he walked off.

"I'm trying to do what's best," said Babar, "but no one understands, except this little warthog."

"He's interfering with your duty as king," said Cornelius. "We should find another home for him."

"I'll never let him go," said Babar.

Outside the palace kitchen stood two suits of elephant armour. An echo rumbled out of the larger one. "As soon as we get that hog back home, I'm going to blockade EVERYTHING! Where is he?"

There was a clank, and Basil looked over to see Muffy attached to the armour's behind. "I think I've found him," he said.

Then Babar appeared. "Let go of my warthog!" he boomed.

Rataxes dashed through a nearby doorway. "But that's the stairs..." called Basil.

Pompadour and Cornelius were counting the last fuschia feathers. "That's it," said Pompadour. "One thousand pounds exactly."

Cornelius stepped forward. "On behalf of His Majesty," he said, "I would like to thank you for your help, patriotism, and your..."

"Fuschia feathers?" suggested Pompadour.

Suddenly Babar's voice rang out. "Guards! Stop that warthog!" Then Rataxes raced into view and landed in the feathers. Babar rushed up and grabbed Muffy.

"You want pomegranates?" roared Rataxes. "Give me that warthog!"

"But what about your feathers?" asked Pompadour.

"Keep them!" said Rataxes, spitting some out. "I want the hog!"

"Forget the pomegranates," said Babar, "I'm keeping him."

"Right," said Rataxes. "In that case..." But then he heard a familiar voice.

It was Lady Rataxes. "Oh Muffy!"

"Muffy?" said Babar, sadly. "It's your warthog?"

"King Babar, name your reward," smiled Lady Rataxes.

"Our pomegranates back," said Babar, promptly, "and an end to all blockades!"

"Done!" said Lady Rataxes.

"Do you know, I still miss that warthog, sighed Babar to Flora. It's hard to say goodbye to something you love."

"But you were laughing while you told me about him," smiled Flora.

"That's because we had a lot of fun together," Babar grinned. "Instead of wasting time missing old friends, we should always remember how good it was to know them."

Flora gave Babar a hug. "I'll remember."

Based on the animated series
"Babar"
a Nelvana-Ellipse Presentation,
a Nelvana Production in Association
with The Clifford Ross Company.

Based on characters created by
Jean and Laurent de Brunhoff.

Carnival
An imprint of the Children's Division
of the Collins Publishing Group
8 Grafton Street, London W1X 3LA

Published by Carnival 1990

ISBN 0 00 193226 8

Printed in Great Britain by
BPCC Paulton Books Limited

This book is set in New Century Schoolbook 14 point